W9-AGY-407

SIMON SPOTLIGHT

An imprint of Simon & Schuster Children's Publishing Division
1230 Avenue of the Americas, New York, New York 10020
This Simon Spotlight hardcover edition October 2016
Copyright © 2016 by Simon & Schuster, Inc. Text by Michael Teitelbaum.
Illustrations by Graham Ross. All rights reserved, including the right of
reproduction in whole or in part in any form.
SIMON SPOTLIGHT and colophon are registered trademarks of
Simon & Schuster, Inc.
For information about special discounts for bulk purchases, please contact
Simon & Schuster Special Sales at 1-866-506-1949 or business@simonandschuster.com.
Designed by Jay Colvin
The text of this book was set in Minya Novelle.
Manufactured in the United States of America 0916 FFG
10 9 8 7 6 5 4 3 2 1
ISBN 978-1-4814-6896-1 (hc)
ISBN 978-1-4814-6895-4 (pbk)
ISBN 978-1-4814-6897-8 (eBook)
Library of Congress Catalog Card Number 2015950426

Chapter One

Definitely Sure

MY NAME IS BILLY SURE. RIGHT NOW I'M SITTING at my workbench at the World Headquarters of **SURE THINGS, INC.** Across the room—which used to be the Reyes family garage—sits my best friend and business partner, Manny Reyes. Manny and I make up Sure Things, Inc., the world's only inventing company run by seventh graders—or so we thought.

We recently discovered that a company named Definite Devices also exists, and it is *also* run by two seventh graders—Nat Definite and Jada Parikh. And not only do they exist, but they were working on an invisibility invention at the same time as us at Sure Things, Inc.!

As you can imagine, that was kind of a problem. But Manny, being the genius chief financial officer (CFO) he is, worked out a deal. We all agreed to jointly release an invisibility kit produced by both Sure Things, Inc. and Definite Devices—the DEFINITELY SURE INVISIBILITY (AND ANTI-INVISIBILITY) SPRAYS.

Before our two companies agreed to work together on that one invention, Nat did her best to try to steal Manny away from me—and from Sure Things, Inc! She wanted him to work with her over at Definite Devices, because . . . well, the obvious answer is that Manny is a brilliant CFO, businessperson, marketing genius, computer whiz . . . but it's MORE THAN THAT.

Nat has a crush on Manny!

"That is the most beautiful spreadsheet I've ever seen, Manny," Nat says, her face glowing. (Oh yeah. Because we're technically partners

2

and all, she's sitting at the World Headquarters now too.)

Jada, who Manny agreed to train as the CFO for Definite Devices, scrunches up her face.

"How can a spreadsheet be beautiful, Nat?" she asks. "It's just a series of numbers and projections and—"

"Anything Manny does is beautiful," says Nat.

See what I mean?

"So, Jada," Manny begins, doing his best to ignore Nat, "as you can see, we've placed the sprays in a few high-end specialty stores."

"To generate early buzz on social media," Jada adds.

"Exactly," Manny replies. "So by the time we release it to the major chains—"

"—people will be waiting in line to buy it," Jada finishes.

Jada's really smart. Like . . . Manny-smart.

Just then a noise comes from Manny's phone. **Ping!**

"Looks like we have another incident of

someone using the Definitely Sure Invisibility Spray to cut a line," Manny says, frowning. "Last week someone used it at a movie theater. Now in a theme park."

"That's not good," I say. Then I get an idea. "Maybe the next batch of sprays can make kids who try to cut lines grow REALLY BIG ELEPHANT TRUNKS! Temporarily, of course."

"Great idea, *partner*," Manny says. "That could make using the rides really hard!"

I might be imagining it, but I think he

emphasizes the word "partner" so that Nat and Jada notice.

"All right, that's enough work for today," Manny adds with a smile.

I think what Manny really means is, *You should go home now, Nat.*

Nat frowns. But she can't complain, because she *has* been here for hours. She and Jada pack up and leave.

I'm just about to do my best Nat imitation a few minutes later, ("Manny, you are so, *so* funny!") when **Briiiiing! Briiiing!** *My* phone rings. I don't recognize the number.

I pick up the phone, hoping it has nothing to do with Definite Devices. Don't get me wrong—I'm happy there are other kids out there who are working on their dreams. I've just kind of had enough of them for today.

"Hi, Billy?" comes a voice through the phone.

Hmm. It doesn't sound like Nat or Jada!

"Is this a good time to talk?" she asks, pronouncing every syllable clearly in a British accent. "It's Gemma Weston."

Gemma... *Weston*?!

She's only the most famous movie star in the whole world!

Chapter Two

TV or Not TV

"UH, HEY, GEMMA, HOW ARE YOU DOING?" I say, thinking instantly that I sound like a major dork. I just so happen to be speaking to one of the world's biggest celebrities, and here I am, saying things like "uh, hey."

"I'm well, thank you," Gemma replies. "I still think about the fun we had filming *Alien Zombie Attack!*"

Okay, explanation. Not too long ago, Manny, Emily, and I were extras in Gemma's film *Alien Zombie Attack!* as part of an agreement to let Sure Things, Inc.'s hovercraft invention be used in the film. While there, Emily and Gemma became close friends. And I hadn't realized it, but I'm now on a first name basis with Gemma Weston too!

"That was pretty fun, Gemma," I say. "I had a really good time making that movie. So, what's up?"

"If you remember, I told you that I'd love to work with Sure Things, Inc. again," Gemma says excitedly. "And the chance to work together has just come up! I've been asked to host a new TV show called *Sing Out and Shout*. It's airing live this weekend. It's a singing competition show."

"A singing competition show," I repeat. "Is it okay if I put you on speakerphone, Gemma? I'm at the Sure Things, Inc. office now, and I'd love to have Manny listen in."

"Absolutely!" Gemma says.

Click. Her voice fills the open air.

"Hello, Manny! I was just telling Billy about a singing competition TV show I'm hosting. We are looking for celebrity contestants and celebrity judges, and I thought that you two might be interested," Gemma explains.

CELEBRITY JUDGES?!

Did the mega movie star Gemma Weston just call me a celebrity? I mean, tons of kids know my name because of my inventions and all that—but enough to be called a celebrity by an *actual* celebrity . . . that's a whole other level of cool!

"So, what do you think?" Gemma asks. "Can I count on you two to help me out this weekend?"

Manny and I exchange looks. The weekend is only a few days away. I'm ready to pipe up and scream YES!, but Manny looks a little concerned.

"Can you give us a second, Gemma?" I ask. I put the call on mute.

"What's the matter?" I ask Manny. "We always have a good time when we go on TV."

"Billy, I don't love being in the spotlight," Manny says. "Every time we've been on TV before, it's you who's been interviewed. I only agreed to be in *Alien Zombie Attack!* because we were dressed as zombies. And for our Next Big Thing show, I was promoting Sure Things, Inc. But for me personally to be on TV—I just don't know. . . ."

Huh. I never realized that Manny has a little bit of stage fright.

"But that's the beautiful thing about this show," I explain. "*We* won't be in the spotlight. The celebrity singers will be. And so this becomes awesome publicity for Sure Things, Inc., just as we are promoting the REALLY GREAT HOVERCRAFT TOY and the INVISIBILITY KIT. And all this, Manny, will be hosted by a big movie star!"

Okay, I guess that was all really Manny of me to say. Manny is usually the one to push publicity on me, but I think this makes sense. Also I *really* want to work with Gemma Weston again. I wouldn't admit this to anyone, but I might have a teeny-tiny crush on Gemma Weston, although it's nowhere near as big as the crush Nat has on Manny.

Manny thinks for a moment, then smiles. I can see him warming to this idea.

"Well, when you put it that way . . . ," he says. "All that publicity. Yeah, let's do it. After all, what can happen?"

"Score!" I shout.

I quickly touch my phone's screen to unmute us.

"Well, that was fast," Gemma says.

"Yeah, it didn't take long for us to figure out that this is a GREAT IDEA. Manny and I would love to be on *Sing Out and Shout*. Sign us up!"

"That's fantastic, Team Sure Things, Inc.," she says. "I just know you two are going to have a great time. And also, one request?" she asks. "Please invite Emily to the show on my behalf. I really miss her. And it's strange—lately it seems that her phone is always off. That's not like Em at all."

I really wasn't kidding when I said Emily and Gemma are close friends.

She's right, of course. Emily's phone *has* been off. That's because she's been grounded.

Remember when I said we were extras on Gemma's film? Well, we weren't supposed to be—a few weeks ago, Emily stole my hover-craft invention and crash-landed at the studio. Dad let us be in the movie, but after Emily's little bout of—you know—STEALING my hovercraft—he grounded her "for life." I don't think he's *too* serious about the "for life" sentence, though, because later he said that if she is as nice as she can possibly be and does ONE NICE BIG THING for everyone in the family, she will be ungrounded.

But until then, no phone. I'm not going to tell Gemma that. Despite the fact that Emily and I don't always get along—did I mention that she's my big sister?—I don't need to embarrass her.

"I'll definitely relay the message, Gemma," I say.

"Great. Thanks. I'll send you the schedule for the show soon. See ya, Billy and Manny!"

"Bye, Gemma," Manny and I say in unison.

Bye, Gemma. How cool is that!

I stand near the door with a huge smile on my face. That's when I notice something—it's really late! I hardly noticed the time passing with everything going on today at the office.

"Uh, I should go home now," I say, feeling a little foolish, standing there in a daze because I just got off the phone with Gemma Weston. "See ya tomorrow, Manny. Come on, Philo!"

My dog, Philo, who always comes with me to the Sure Things, Inc. office, follows me out the door. I hop onto my bike and head for home.

At home I run into Emily in the upstairs hallway. Or at least, I *think* I run into Emily. It could also be a FLAMINGO. Or a TINY, FLUFFY DOG. Or an OSTRICH. But since none of those options really make sense, I

decide it's Emily wearing a really strange-look-ing hat. The hat has three flowers growing out the front and a statue of a bird with its wings spread open on the back.

This? This has *got* to be Emily's next "thing." My sister has always had a "thing," like speaking with a British accent, or wearing glasses with no lenses, or apparently wearing a hat that makes her look like a flamingo-dog-ostrich hybrid. Thankfully, Emily's things are gone as quickly as they come. And for her sake, I'm hoping this one goes *fast*.

"You're never going to believe who called me today," I begin, doing my best not to laugh.

"Dad?" Emily replies. "Saying I'm ungrounded and can have my phone back?"

"Sorry, no," I say. "It was Gemma Weston!"

Emily's expression immediately changes. "She called *you*? Why did she call you?"

"She asked Manny and me to be on her new TV show. Isn't that cool?"

Emily's eyes flash. Emily is Sure Things, Inc.'s VERY OFFICIAL HOLLYWOOD

14

COORDINATOR, so technically, booking a TV show falls into her realm of business at Sure Things, Inc. But I think she's so upset about her phone—or maybe she's so tired from wearing that heavy hat all day—that she doesn't say anything.

I continue. "And Gemma invited you to come to the TV show as her special guest, too," I say. "But it airs this weekend . . ."

"No! That does it!" Emily screeches. "I have *got* to get out of this grounded-for-life punishment by then!"

She storms into her room and slams the door shut.

You're welcome, I think.

Chapter Three

Making Things Write

AT DINNER I'M ABSOLUTELY BUZZING ABOUT THE TV show. I just hope that Mom has convinced Dad to order in food tonight.

My dad is great. He's a fabulous father and a pretty good artist (even if "pretty good artist" means he loves painting close-ups of Philo's tongue). What he is not, however, is a good cook.

I sit down at the table. *Oh no,* I think. The Sure family silverware is out. That means we aren't using plastic silverware, which means Mom probably didn't order in. . . .

"Good news," Dad announces as he sits down. "I

made a brand-new dish—roasted kale roots casserole with caramel syrup and cottage cheese! I thought it up myself!"

I certainly can't imagine anyone else thinking it up. And, as always, I'm thankful for Sure Things, Inc.'s GROSS-TO-GOOD POWDER. It does exactly what it sounds like it does—makes gross food taste good—and it's kept hidden in the salt shaker at the family table so we don't hurt Dad's feelings.

A few seconds later Emily comes downstairs and sits next to me. She's wearing a new hat with multicolored feathers sticking out in every direction.

Philo takes one look at Emily's hat, groans, and runs behind the couch.

Dad places the casserole dish onto a square metal trivet on the table. Without saying a word, he globs his creation onto each of our plates. Mom, Emily, and I all reach for the salt shaker containing Gross-to-Good-Powder at the same time.

"I think I might make this dish the subject

of my next painting," Dad announces.

I look down at the casserole. It's pretty goopy. I don't know much about art, but it looks like the FARTHEST THING FROM ART to me.

"I'm so proud of you, Bryan," says Mom. "Tons of people showed up for your art show, and their reactions were wonderful."

"I bet it was funny watching those artsy folks debate what they were looking at, while you knew it was really a painting of Philo's nose!" I say to Dad.

"As long as they enjoyed the paintings, they're allowed to think whatever they like," Dad says. "That's the beauty of art. Each person has his or her own interpretation."

How can you not know you are looking at a dog nose? I think. But I don't say anything.

As if to change the subject, Mom turns to Emily and me. "How were your days?" she asks.

"Great, actually," I say, answering first. The more I get to talk, the less I have to eat. "I got a phone call from Gemma Weston!"

"Wow!" says Mom. "Em, didn't you two really hit it off when you shot that vampire movie?"

Emily looks at Mom. I can't figure out if the tortured expression on her face is because she wasn't able to get Gemma's call directly or because Mom can't tell the difference between vampires and zombies.

"Zombies, Mom," says Emily, brushing feathers out of her eyes. One feather pops loose and floats down, landing in her dinner.

"The movie was about zombies," Emily continues.

It's silent for a second.

"Right. Zombies, of course," Mom says. She turns to me. "So what did Gemma want?"

I fill everyone in on the details of the *Sing Out and Shout* TV show.

"That's fantastic, Billy," says Dad. "Another TV show—my son, the TV star!"

I see a sly smile spread across Emily's face. I can almost see her brain working. If she slips in something fast about going to the TV show too, Mom and Dad might forget she's grounded!

"You left out the best part, Billy," Emily says. "My close friend Gemma has personally invited me to go to the show as her SPECIAL GUEST. Isn't that exciting?"

Yup, I saw that one coming.

But unfortunately for Emily, Mom is a spy—which means she picks up on every detail.

"You, young lady, are still grounded," Mom points out. "Remember?"

Emily sighs. "How could I forget?" She mumbles under her breath.

"You still have one nice thing to do for Dad, and then your punishment will be over," Mom says.

"I just wish there was something I could help Dad with," Emily says, looking down at her food and noticing the feather on her plate for the first time. "I can't exactly help him cook. We all know our . . . cooking preferences . . . are, um, different."

Nice save, Em. I was wondering where she was headed with that.

Dad, who seems to genuinely want to help Emily out, stops shoveling his dinner into his mouth and scratches his head. I can almost see *his* brain working as he searches for something nice Emily can do for him.

"I'VE GOT IT!" he exclaims a few seconds later. "Em, why don't you help me write the thank-you notes to the people who came to my art show? I was going to type them all, but a handwritten card is just so much more personal. And thankfully, I kept a list of everyone who came!"

Emily looks up excitedly.

"Sure, Dad!" she says, her whole mood instantly brightening. "So that means when I'm done, my grounded-for-life status is finished?" Truthfully, I'm wondering the same thing. Did she really get off so easy?

Mom and Dad shrug.

"I don't see why not," Mom says.

"You can get started on them tonight," says Dad cheerily. "Only FIVE THOUSAND THREE HUNDRED AND EIGHTY-TWO thank-you notes to go!"

Chapter Four

Pen Pal

I'M AT THE OFFICE THE NEXT DAY WHEN I GET AN e-mail from Gemma, outlining the details for *Sing Out and Shout*. Which is pretty good, considering the taping starts in two days.

Manny joins me as I open the e-mail.

"Okay, it looks like the show is going to be a three-day extravaganza, broadcast live on Friday, Saturday, and Sunday," I say.

We dive into the meat of the e-mail:

Hey, Billy and Manny, I am so excited that you have both agreed to take part in

Sing Out and Shout. As a reminder, *Sing Out and Shout* is a reality show where celebrities who aren't famous for their music compete to see who is the best singer! Here are the rules:

Six celebrities will compete. Two celebrities will be sent home after the first night, two after the second night, and on the third night the remaining two contenders will sing a duet, but only one will be crowned the *Sing Out and Shout* champion.

Sing Out and Shout will be judged by three celebrity judges as well as viewers at home (home viewers will send in their votes through text message).

The winner of *Sing Out and Shout* will choose a charity and donate the prize money to it.

"This sound great, doesn't it, Manny?" I say when we finish reading. "I think we're going to have a blast on this show. I wonder who the celebrity singers will be."

"Sounds like fun," Manny says calmly. Then he turns back to his sales figures. I don't say anything, but I think Manny is a little nervous.

That night at home as I head upstairs, I pass Emily's room. I see a small pile of completed notes on one side of her desk and a huge stack of blank notepaper piled up on the other side.

All the notes Emily has written

All the notes Emily still has to write

And, of course, she's wearing a hat. Tonight's hat looks like a bright-orange flying saucer stuck to the side of her head. Well, at least it doesn't have any feathers.

"How's it going?" I ask, genuinely concerned that she might not be able to go to the TV show. Emily may be my annoying older sister, but I know how much it means to her.

Emily just nods and mumbles "okay" without even looking up. She finishes one card, adds it to the smaller pile, then grabs the next blank one.

"It's tougher than it looks, huh?" I ask sympathetically.

"It's a *lot* of work, Billy," she says. "Look at this."

She picks up the guestbook that Dad put out at his art show. "Some of these people only wrote their names in the guestbook. No mailing address, no e-mail address, no phone number, no nothing! Fortunately, I'm good at tracking people down—but still, I don't know how I'm going to finish in time to go to the TV show."

I decide not to point out that the last time Emily bragged about being good at tracking people down, she wasn't able to figure out who Nat Definite was.

"Like, look at this!" Emily continues, pointing to a page in the guestbook. "This person, TALI DECISO? All she wrote was

her name. No address, phone, e-mail, nothing! Where do I even start to look to track her down? I know that Dad had visitors at the show from all over the world. What if she's from a different country? This is really hard."

I admit it. I feel bad for Emily. I know how much she wants to go to the TV show. And this does look like an almost impossible task.

"Good luck, Em," I say, then I head to my room.

Emily grunts and goes back to writing.

I wish I could help somehow, but my handwriting isn't very neat. If I'm being honest, it kind of looks like a sea monster's

handwriting—if the sea monster had no arms!

Hmm. Wait a minute. That gives me an idea. (No, not creating an army of sea monsters—though that would be awesome.) Maybe I *can* help Emily! I may not have neat handwriting, but I do have pretty neat inventing skills . . . and I bet I can make a special pen that will help her finish the job faster.

But now comes the hard part—inventing!

The next day I get to the office feeling pretty energized. It's been a long time since I've invented something for fun. Don't get me wrong, inventing *is* fun, and I need to get this right ASAP to help Emily out—but it's been a while since I've been able to tinker around with parts and pieces, rather than trying to roll out the Next Big Thing!

I draw a couple of rough sketches for what the special pen can be, but nothing seems to be coming together. I draw and draw and draw, until . . .

Craaaaash!

I move my arm so quickly across the page that I accidentally knock over my cup of pencils. Pencils fly out, scratching their way across the sketch pad. I glance down and see six identical gray lines all curving in the same direction.

BINGO!

I can almost see the giant lightbulb appear above my head. That's it! Emily's special pen will be able to write many notes at the same time! And I think I have just the parts and pieces to make this invention.

"Hey, Manny," I call across the room.

Manny is firing off e-mails to get more publicity for our TV show appearance.

"Remember when you bought a big box of MANNEQUIN HANDS?" I ask.

Okay, there was a brief period of time where Manny kept ordering some pretty kooky supplies online. I used to make fun of them . . . but now I see they can come in, dare I say, HANDY!

"Funny, I was just thinking about those fake hands," Manny replies.

"Really?"

"Nah." Manny laughs. "But what about them? Do you think they could be contestants on *Sing Out and Shout?*"

Now I laugh, thinking about all of those hands performing a song!

"I have an idea to make a special pen for

Emily that will help her write thank-you notes," I explain. "And those hands would be perfect to work with! Do you know where they are?"

Manny shakes his head. That means I'll have to start looking around the office for the fake hands . . . which *also* means I'm going to come across a ton of the other supplies he ordered.

I start with a heavy-looking box in the corner. Thankfully Manny is much more organized than I am—there's no order to how the boxes are set up, but at least there are labels.

I thumb my way across BROKEN WINDSHIELD WIPERS, TACO HOLDERS, USED DENTURES, and INSIDE-OUT UMBRELLAS. Then next to RUBBER CHICKENS are the mannequin hands! I grab the box and hurry back to my workbench.

Now here comes the fun part.

I line up ten hands and slip a pen into each one, attaching them all together with some other parts and pieces so they're all controlled by one pen in the center. That pen is powered by your own hand, so it writes the same note eleven times at once!

Okay, I'm ready to test this.

I line up blank pieces of paper and start writing.

> Dear Art Lover,
>
> I'm so glad you came to my art show. I thank you, my family thanks you, but most importantly, Philo's butt thanks you.
>
> Many thanks,
>
> Bryan Sure

It works! Each pen moves as my own pen does and writes on the blank sheets of paper. The notes are all written in fresh ink and look perfect! Well, as perfect as my handwriting can look. . . .

"Hey, Manny, check this out!" I say.

Manny touches his phone, sending off one more e-mail, then joins me at my workbench.

"Watch this."

I demo the invention for him by drawing a doodle of a microphone. The doodle gets copied ten times.

"It's the 11-IN-1 PEN!" I announce, smiling.

"This is awesome, partner," Manny says. He smiles too. "Emily is going to love it."

Manny heads back to his desk as I pack up for the day. I'm feeling really good. I didn't even have to sleep-invent (sometimes, when I'm working on an invention, I wake up and find the blueprints at my desk). But more than that, if Emily can get her work done ten times as fast, she can probably come with us to the TV show taping. As much as I'm *not* looking forward to hearing "Em" and "Gem" scream each other's names when they see each other, I really don't want Emily to miss out.

"See you tomorrow!" Manny says as I head out the door. "Right after school so we can leave for the studio."

I smile. I've been so excited to help Emily,

I almost forgot our first studio day is tomorrow! It's kind of like that exciting "first day of school feeling," but more exciting because instead of getting homework, we'll get to be on TV!

Chapter Five

Lend Me a Hand

AS SOON AS I GET HOME, I HURRY TO EMILY'S ROOM.
There she is, scribbling away, one note at a time.
On her head sits a hat that looks like a yellow
pigeon landed on some green cauliflower. I'm
beginning to sense a bird theme with these
strange hats.

"Any luck on finding that Tali DeCiso
person?" I ask.

Emily looks up from her desk.

"As a matter of fact, yes," Emily says.
"As I suspected, she lives in another country.
I managed to track down her e-mail address,

and found out she works at the RAFFREDDARE GALLERY in Rome, one of the top art museums in all of Italy!"

"I'm impressed," I say. "Impressed that you tracked her down, but also impressed that someone so important in the art world would be interested in a painting of Philo's tongue!"

"Yeah," Emily mumbles as she goes back to writing. I can see she wants me to leave.

"I brought you something," I say.

"Uh-huh," she replies, too exhausted to either care what I have to say or to tell me to go away.

"Look!" I insist. I hold out the 11-in-1 Pen that was hiding behind my back. It spins and the hands spin with it.

Emily's eyes go wide.

"What. Is. That. Thing?!" she nearly barks, horrified.

I take another glance at the 11-in-1 Pen. One of the hands droops out at me. Okay, I can see now why Manny didn't suggest Sure Things, Inc. manufacture this one. It looks a little scary. But still, it's really cool!

"Here, I'll show you how it works," I say. "Can you grab me eleven blank thank-you cards?"

"You had these mannequin hands just sitting around?" Emily asks, eyeing the contraption suspiciously.

"Yes," I reply, matter-of-fact.

Emily shrugs. She grabs eleven cards.

"So what happens now?" she asks. "Is this thing going to come to life and help write the cards for me?"

"Not exactly," I explain. "*You're* going to help yourself with these cards! That way, when Dad asks if you did it, you really won't be lying. Line up eleven blank notes. Then write on the middle one and watch what happens."

Emily follows my instructions. When she finishes writing the note, she looks around and sees eleven completed notes, all looking as if they were individually written—which I guess they were, if you think about it in a certain way.

"Billy, this is fantastic!" Emily says, smiling for the first time in days. "Thank you! Thank you! Thank you!" she cries. Then she gets back to work, writing eleven notes at a time.

A few hours later there's a squeal down the hall.

"I did it! I did it! I did it!" Emily yelps. "I'm going to *Sing Out and Shout!* I did it! I'm FREE!"

I feel really good about helping Emily out, and even better about the upcoming TV show. I'm just so excited! I'm finally getting all the perks of being a famous inventor without the pressure.

I decide to treat myself to some CELEBRA-TORY MILK AND COOKIES in the kitchen, when I walk past my parents' bedroom. The door is open a crack, and I can hear them talking.

"You can't just pack up and go to Italy, Bryan," Mom says.

Italy? Dad is going to Italy?

"And even if you only go for a few months, I can't be sure that *I* won't have to spring into action and leave too," Mom continues, "the kids are not old enough to be left alone."

Left alone? For months? This is very strange. I mean, I got used to Mom being away a lot. (Since she's a spy working for the government, she's often away on assignments.) But both Mom *and* Dad?!

I hear Dad sigh.

"I know," he says. "But this art dealer—Tali DeCiso . . . it sounds like she's offering me an amazing opportunity."

Tali DeCiso! The person that Emily tracked down. She must have gotten in touch with Dad! This is getting stranger by the second.

"I know, Bryan," Mom says softly. "It does sound like a fabulous opportunity. Being commissioned to paint for one of the most famous museums in all of Italy! I realize that this could be a once in a lifetime opportunity for you, and I know how much you would love to do this, but what about Billy and Emily?"

Yeah, what about us? For the first time in a long time, I'm feeling more than a little worried.

Chapter Six

Showtime!

THE BIG DAY FINALLY ARRIVES.

I float through my school day wondering if anyone notices. I'm so tired that I end up taking a power nap during lunch. But it works out, because I feel much more energetic when it's time to head over to the TV studio!

Mom, Dad, Manny, Manny's parents, and I pile into the Reyes family SUV. I sit pretty cramped in the back row, sandwiched between Manny and my dad. It's not until we are half-way to the studio that I realize Emily is not with us.

"Hey, WHAT ABOUT EMILY?" I ask.

Mom and Dad shrug.

"She didn't want to come with us," Dad says distractedly.

Okay, that's weird. Who drove Emily to the studio?

But I don't have a lot of time to think about this, because soon I'm walking through the glass doors leading to the TV studio, getting a familiar TV show thrill! As weird as it is, I feel comfortable here. This is where Manny and I did the *Next Big Thing* TV show to help us pick the NO-TROUBLE BUBBLE as a Sure Things, Inc. invention. There's a picture of me on the wall. It's kind of like my HOME AWAY FROM HOME.

Kind of.

If my home had superstar celebrities waltzing around!

I spot Gemma Weston walking down the hall toward us.

She has a big smile on her face, and she's waving her hand broadly over her head.

Wow! I didn't realize that Gemma would be

so happy to see me again. That's pretty cool.

Gemma is only a couple of feet away now. I'm about to say hi when she lets out a loud squeal.

"Em!" she shrieks.

A voice from behind me shrieks back: "Gem!"

I spin around and see Emily rushing into the building. Before I can even start to wonder how she got here, I see that she has selected her most outrageous hat to wear to the TV show. And that's *saying something*. It is bright purple with ribbons all over it . . . and some CRAZY giant googly eyes extending from antennae coming out of the top! But no bird theme this time. Interesting.

Emily rushes past Dad, Manny, Manny's parents, and me, and gives Gemma a big hug.

"It is sooooo great to see you, Gem!" Emily exclaims. "Thank you so much for inviting me!"

"You look *fabulous*, Em!" Gemma says. "I absolutely *love* that hat! You have to tell me where you got it."

"And you have to tell me how you got here—" I start to say, genuinely curious, when all of a sudden a CHAUFFEUR walks inside, wearing a uniform and all!

"Miss Emily, you forgot your handbag," the chauffeur says, handing Emily a bright purple handbag with ribbons and googly eyes all over it.

Emily takes it and smiles.

"Thanks so much for picking up Emily,

Hector," Gemma says. "You're the best."

Hector nods, then walks back outside . . . to where a GIANT limo is parked!

Hold up. I help Emily get ungrounded, and *she's* the one who gets to arrive in a fancy car?

I don't have time to complain though, because Gemma turns to the rest of us. "Come on. I'll take you on a tour of the studio before we get started," she says. "I know you've all been here before, but studios adapt to whatever show is taping that day. Showbiz is anything but boring."

Gemma leads all of us through the large studio where the show will take place. Production assistants scurry everywhere, pushing large TV cameras, dragging thick wires, and hanging huge lights.

Gemma takes us into a conference room. There, a small teenage girl with straight dark hair sits at a piano.

"Everyone, I'd like you to meet YAMUNA STONE," Gemma says. "She's the musical director of the TV show, and she'll be writing brand-new original songs for every contestant."

Yamuna smiles at all of us, and takes a long look at Emily's hat and bag. If she thinks they're weird, she doesn't say anything.

I didn't think we could meet any celebrity bigger than Gemma Weston, but wow—Yamuna Stone! Her face has been on the cover of every music magazine there is. This just keeps getting better and better!

"I love your music," says Emily. If she's

star struck, she doesn't show it. But I guess now that Emily is friends with the likes of Gemma Weston, nothing else can faze her.

"This is Manny Reyes, one half of Sure Things, Inc.," Gemma says.

Manny and Yamuna shake hands.

"Very nice to meet you," says Manny.

"And this is Billy Sure," Gemma says, gesturing to me.

I shake Yamuna's hand. "I am a big fan," I say.

"So am I, Billy," says Yamuna, much to my surprise. "I have one of the first edition ALL BALLS. I still like to toss it around with my songwriting partners when we get stuck creatively."

I'm picturing a bunch of celebrities using some of Sure Things, Inc.'s inventions. Maybe the famous Jelsen twins have tried the SIBLING SILENCER on each other. Or Yamuna Stone could write eleven copies of a new song at once with the 11-in-1 Pen!

"I'm really looking forward to writing for

both of you," Yamuna says to Manny and me.

"Thanks," I say automatically.

Then I think for a moment. Why is Yamuna talking about writing for us? Maybe she wants to write a jingle for Sure Things, Inc.'s next commercial? Hmm, that must be it. Maybe Manny was able to swing that in one of his many marketing e-mails. Awesome.

"Okay, gang, let's keep moving," says Gemma.

She leads us into the green room, which is where performers wait before they go on the air.

Sitting in the room on a long couch are the contestants who will be competing on the program.

I see Dad's eyes open wide.

"This is Arthur Ling," Gemma says. "He's a—"

"Famous TV chef!" Dad finishes her sentence. "I've gotten some of my best recipes from watching his show!"

Arthur is a tall teenager who gives Dad a big smile.

"Wait until you see what I'm starting to do with PICKLED ANCHOVIES!" Arthur says. "It's fabulous!"

"Oh boy," says Dad. "I'll have to watch and then work them into my next meal."

Emily, Mom, and I all exchange looks, but, of course, we say nothing.

"Are all of you part of the show?" asks Arthur.

"I'm Emily, and I'm Gemma's *personal friend*," Emily explains, emphasizing "personal friend." "These are my mom and dad; my brother, Billy; his business partner, Manny, and Manny's parents. Billy and Manny are going to be part of the show."

"Nice to meet you all," says Arthur.

I instantly like Arthur. Okay, maybe I don't like that he gives Dad some pretty bad cooking ideas, but I like how comfortable he makes me feel. I've known Arthur for all of two seconds, and I already feel like he's easy to talk to. I hope he's just as good at singing!

"And this is Sarina Brown," says Gemma,

pointing to a girl who seems to be about my age. "She's a makeup artist."

Emily's face lights up, though it's a bit hard to see behind her hat!

"I subscribe to all of your beauty videos," she says. "I *love* them! Especially when your dog makes a guest appearance. Like when you

let him sniff out which lipstick you should wear!"

Sarina smiles. "Copper always chooses the best lipstick," she says. "And I'm always happy to meet a fan."

"I can't wait to hear you sing!" Emily tells her.

I'm about to ask just how Copper can help Sarina sniff out makeup since I'm pretty sure she doesn't use the CAT-DOG TRANSLATOR, when Gemma leads us away, this time to a tall kid dressed in a glittery shirt. He leaps up from the couch, spins on his toes, then extends his hand.

"Meet Marcus Rebu," Gemma says, seeming to be as surprised by Marcus's little spin move as the rest of us are. "He's a backup dancer for Dustin Peeler."

"Very nice to meet you all," says Marcus, spinning back in the other direction.

I can see Manny's mom, who is a podiatrist, stare at his feet. It's like she has a zoom-in camera on them.

"You can make your feet more flexible by giving your toes a workout, like picking up pencils or ANCHOVIES off the floor!" she says all too cheerfully for someone talking about *both* feet and anchovies.

Marcus smiles at her kindly, but poor Manny's face turns bright red.

"One more contestant for you guys to meet," says Gemma, sensing the awkward interaction afoot.

She leads us around a corner in the green room. There, sitting on a wooden chair at a desk jotting down notes, is none other than NAT DEFINITE!

"Hey, guys!" says Nat. "Long time no see, huh?"

I'm stunned. No, stunned doesn't even begin to cover it. I'm . . . I'm whatever is more stunned than stunned.

"You're singing?" I ask.

"Yup, why not?" Nat says. "I guess all the publicity from our invisibility product helped me earn a place in this competition." Then she turns and looks right at Manny.

"Hi, Manny. It's *wonderful* to see you."

Manny waves meekly. I can tell he is also not happy to see Nat here.

I wish Nat wouldn't be so obvious about her crush on Manny—especially with other people around.

Then I think of something else. Is it fair for Manny and me to be judges since we know one of the contestants? But then again, Gemma personally invited Manny and me to judge, so it's probably okay. . . .

Speaking of Gemma, she puts her arms around Manny and me.

"Let's go meet the judges," she says. "Everyone else, make yourself comfortable here in the green room. Help yourself to some snacks."

Mom, Dad, Dr. Reyes, Mr. Reyes, and Emily eye one another, then dive right into the colorful jelly beans on the counter.

As I follow Gemma out of the green room, I feel a bit confused. Gemma's e-mail said there were going to be *six* contestants, but we've only met four. Maybe the other two haven't gotten here yet?

Manny and I follow Gemma back to the studio. The far wall has a long table. Two people are sitting there beside one empty chair.

"Billy, Manny, these are the judges," Gemma says. "Meet Dustin Peeler."

Dustin, who has close-cropped blond hair, reaches over and shakes my hand.

"Nice to see you again, Team Sure Things, Inc.," Dustin says.

We met Dustin when we were guests on the TV show *Better Than Sleeping!* We found out at that time that he was a big fan of the All Ball. Okay, so I guess it's all right if we know Nat, because Dustin definitely knows his backup dancer, Marcus. That makes me feel better.

"And our next judge is Nicholas Campbell," Gemma says. "He writes for all the TOP MUSIC MAGAZINES."

Nicholas nods in our direction but doesn't

say a word. I've heard of Nicholas Campbell. He has a reputation for being a really tough critic. He also doesn't seem friendly at all. I get a feeling I'm not really going to like working with this guy.

That's when I notice that there is only one empty chair at the judges' table, and—based on the giant sign that says GEMMA—that one's for Gemma.

"Um," I say nervously, pointing to the table. Has there been a mistake? Are we not going to be on the TV show after all? I start to feel a pit forming in my stomach.

"Where do Manny and I sit?" I ask.

Gemma tilts her head and looks at us strangely.

"What do you mean?" she says.

Gemma looks into my confused face and her eyes widen. It's like the answer has suddenly become clear.

"Oh!" she says, laughing hard now. I can't help but think, *What's so funny?* Was this all a prank? What's going on?

"Billy, you two aren't guest judges," Gemma says in between laughs.

"We're *not*?"

Worst fear: CONFIRMED!

"Then why are we here?"

"You two are *contestants!*" Gemma announces.

Chapter Seven

Billy Sure, Singer???

I LOOK OVER AT MANNY. HE'S ALREADY STARING AT me in shock.

Contestants? Us? Contestants?

No, no, no . . . I do not sing. I can't sing. I'm a terrible singer. Asking me to sing is like asking Philo to do my homework. It's just a mistake.

"I don't know about this, Gemma," I say. "I'm not really a good singer."

"None of the celebrities are professional singers," Gemma points out. "They're here, like you guys, to help out, have some fun, and raise money for charity."

I look at Manny. He tilts his head and raises his eyebrows.

I know that look. It means: *She does have a point.*

Then I remember Gemma's e-mail about the rules, and another unpleasant thought pops into my head!

"But only one person can win *Sing Out and Shout*," I say. "Does that mean Manny and I will have to compete against each other?"

Gemma nods. "Yup. Only one person can be the winner."

Mayday. MAYDAY!

I'm starting to get really nervous here.

"Well, in reality you're both just competing *for charity*," Gemma continues, emphasizing the charity part. "And I think the Young Inventors Organization could be the perfect charity for you to donate to, if one of you wins. They're an organization that helps kids invent. A big donation could really save them—without a donation soon they might have to close down."

No pressure, I guess. . . .

"So it's all in good fun, and the real winners are the charities, right?" Gemma says, flashing her hundred-watt smile.

"That makes sense," Manny agrees. "Don't you think, Billy?"

I see immediately that there really is no way out of this. I already told Gemma I'd do it. Manny's already told newspapers and websites and even the school paper we'd do it. I'm going to have to sing on TV no matter how big a fool I make of myself.

But I can't get out any words. So I just nod.

"EXCELLENT!" says Gemma. "I've got a few last minute details to take care of backstage. Why don't you two join the other contestants in the green room?"

With that, she turns and hurries away.

As soon as she disappears from sight, Manny puts his hand on my shoulder.

"Here's the thing, Billy," he says. "Aside from charity, if we both make it to the final round as the last two contestants, it would be some really great publicity for Sure Things, Inc. Much more than if only one of us makes it. Which means we'll sell a lot more of our products if we both make it to the end. Doesn't that make sense?"

I realize now that Manny has never heard me sing. There's a reason for that. No one has ever heard me sing except Philo, and he always runs out of the room. Of course, I haven't heard Manny sing either, but for some reason he doesn't seem worried about opening his mouth in front of millions of people on TV. Maybe I should be more like

Manny. And like Gemma said, it's all in good fun. . . .

"I'll try my best," I finally say.

On our way back to the green room, I happen to glance up at the technical booth, where the lighting and sound people make their magic happen. There, chatting with one of the technicians, is Nat.

It's weird that a contestant is up there, but I don't think much else of it.

By the time Manny and I get back to the green room, Mom, Dad, Manny's parents, and Emily have left. The production assistant at the door tells me that they went to get seats before the show begins. They will all be watching from the studio audience.

Yamuna asks all of the contestants to gather round, and we do. She is very short, but knows how to command the room. I'm impressed!

"Okay, now that we're all here, let me explain what's going to happen," Yamuna says. "I'll be writing individual songs for each of you, based on who you are, what you do, and your individual personalities." She smiles. "Just remember, that's the key word here—personality. None of you are professional singers. That's not what this show is about. This show is about the viewing audience getting to know you. That's why we call this reality TV!"

Well, that makes me feel a little better.

Yamuna continues. "The first time you appear onstage, the people watching are going to want to see your personality shine through. They're going to want to meet you in a certain way, as if they are getting an inside glimpse into who their favorite celebrities really are. People always ask me what I do on my days off. This is your opportunity to *show* them what a day in your life is like. You've got to win the audience over before you sing even a single note."

Hmm. That makes sense. Maybe if I can get the audience to like me before I sing, they won't notice how bad a singer I am. And then Manny and I can be the last two contestants standing, and we will be guaranteed to donate the prize money to the Young Inventors Organization!

"So let's get started," Yamuna says. "I'm going to call each of you into the rehearsal studio, one by one, so you can work with me individually on your song. I won't expect you to remember the lyrics, so they'll be available karaoke-style on a screen offstage. Manny, why don't we start with you?"

Manny steps forward.

"See ya, partner," he says to me. "Good luck!" He follows Yamuna into the rehearsal studio.

Meanwhile, I join Arthur, Sarina, Marcus, and Nat on the cushy green room couches. Everyone is a little quiet.

"Anyone else nervous about singing?" I ask.

Good icebreaker, Billy, I think. Way to be MR. COOL.

"You know, Billy, I never even thought about singing," Marcus says. "I always focused on my dancing. So, yeah, I guess I am little nervous."

"I know what you mean," I say. "I'm not only competing against my best friend and

CFO, but Nat here is also a business partner of mine, as well as a competitor."

Everyone stares at me blankly.

"Um, it's a long story," I say.

"Well, I think singing is a lot like cooking," says Arthur. "You must think about all the individual ingredients—the tone of your voice, the lyrics of the song, the feel of your costume—all of it. Then, like in a great meal, you must combine these ingredients carefully, and in the right proportions, so that the flavors blend perfectly."

I can definitely see why Dad likes this guy. If there's one thing Dad likes to do it's mix up individual ingredients—whether they go together or not!

Sarina speaks next. "I like what Yamuna said about showing your personality. That's what I try to do when I put makeup on someone. I use colors and shades, not to hide, but to bring out the REAL PERSON. And that's what I'll be doing when I sing."

Some of the contestants have really been

thinking about this. I have no idea what I'm doing or how to show the "real me." The real me would probably be hunched over my workbench. Or sleep inventing!

"What about you, Nat?" I ask. "Are you nervous? I mean, you don't seem like the nervous type."

"I'm pretty confident," Nat admits. "But, you already know that. Why are you nervous, Billy?"

I really don't want anyone to know that up until five minutes ago I thought I was going to be one of the judges. That would be embarrassing.

"Well, I've never sung in public before, so I guess that makes me a little nervous," I admit.

"Nothing to it," says Nat. "You just set your mind on what you want and go for it!"

That's Nat. Enough confidence for everyone in the room.

The door to the rehearsal studio opens and out comes Manny. In his place, Arthur walks in.

Manny joins us on the green room couches and sprawls out.

"So, how'd it go?" I ask Manny.

"Pretty good," he says. "Yamuna is terrific. Very patient. And she wrote a pretty cool song for me to sing. She obviously did her homework about who we are and what we do. I think you're going to be just fine, Billy."

It goes on like that—each person in and out of the rehearsal studio—until finally . . .

"Billy!" Yamuna calls in a chipper tone. "Your turn."

My hands start shaking. Oh no. My hands shake when I'm nervous. Somehow I manage to get up. I can't really feel my legs. I stomp into the rehearsal studio, one, two, one, two, one, two. . . .

The studio is smaller than I would have guessed. The walls and ceiling are covered in soundproof tiles. There's some recording equipment and a few pictures of elephants. I wonder if Yamuna likes them or something.

Yamuna sits down at a large piano and smiles.

"I can see that you're nervous, Billy," she says. "No worries. Let me reassure you that first, all of your fellow contestants are nervous too."

"Even Manny?" I ask. "I don't think I've ever seen Manny nervous. At least, not that he's shown."

"EVEN MANNY," she says. "It's natural. This is new for all of you."

I feel calmer than at any time since Gemma told me I'd be singing. I can see why Yamuna is so successful. She's really good at her job. And I haven't even heard the song she wrote for me.

"Before we talk about your song, I want to say again that the most important thing you can do out there on that stage is to show the audience what's special and unique about you."

I nod, though I'm not really sure how I'm going to do that.

"I know that there's another kid inventor on this show," Yamuna continues. "*And*, of course, your business partner. But just because you're good at the same thing doesn't mean you're the same person."

You can say that again!

"Neither of them are exactly like you, Billy. Show your humor and likability to the audience and to the judges. The winner of this show will use his or her special talent to win—and, you might be surprised to hear this, but your special talent might not even be singing. The competition is just for fun and the most important thing is that the judges and the audience love you."

You know what? Yamuna is right. I'm starting to feel better about all this.

"Now, let's try out your song," she says, handing me a sheet with lyrics on it. She starts playing the piano. Thankfully the tune is easy to follow.

I take a breath and start to sing:

"I'm so suuuuure about inventing;
I'm real suuuuure about creating.
I can put together what doesn't seem plain.
If you ask me how I do it, I'd be glad to explain.

I am suuuuure about the inventions I'm bringing.
But I want to tell you now, I'm not suuuuure . . .
About SINGING!"

As I sing out the final note, my voice **CRACKS!**
I sound like a chipmunk whistling between his
two front teeth.

Before I can say anything, Yamuna smiles.

"That's okay," she says. "Just go out on stage, sing this song, and make people laugh. You may score pretty low with the judges on the stage, but most of the votes come from the TV viewers anyway. Just go out there, use your special talent, and make yourself lovable! I know you can do it. I'm going to work on a couple more verses for the actual performance."

"Thanks," I say. Then I leave the rehearsal studio.

"How was it?" Manny asks back in the green room.

"Not as bad as I thought," I reply. I don't need to tell Manny about that last note.

Manny checks his watch.

"Looks like we have a little time to practice our songs," he says.

I look around the green room and see all the contestants practicing by themselves. Manny sits down next to me.

"All right, let's hear your song first," I say.

Manny takes a breath and then starts to sing:

"My name is Manny.
My skills are quite uncanny.
I can crunch the numbers, make a marketing plan-y.
I'm the business genius, I'm the mega-money man-ny.
There is no question, there is no doubt,
I am super psyched to be on Sing Out and Shout!"

My mouth drops open. No. Way. MANNY?! Manny, my best friend—my business partner—is absolutely, 100 percent, an INCREDIBLE singer!!!

Chapter Eight

Lights, Camera, Sing Out . . .

"MANNY!" I SHOUT. "YOU CAN PROBABLY WIN THIS thing!"

Manny shrugs, clearly embarrassed, even in front of me . . . but there is no doubt in my mind. Manny can *sing*.

I feel really bad admitting it, but knowing Manny can sing makes me even more nervous. I thought we were both just clueless seventh graders on a reality singing show. Just two kids trying to make it to the end of the competition. But now that I know Manny can sing . . . it makes me a little jealous. I'm certainly not going to win, but Manny could.

A few moments later, Gemma pokes her head into the green room.

"All right, everyone. It's showtime," she says. "I'm going to head onstage, then bring each of you on one by one. Good luck!"

She scurries out and tells us that we can watch the show on the giant monitor in the green room. Just as I'm about to ask where the monitor is, it drops down from the ceiling! An ENORMOUS TV screen fills the wall! Then, just like that, the screen goes dark and the spotlights pop on, sweeping left and right, up and down.

An announcer with a really deep voice speaks: "Good evening, and welcome to *Sing Out and Shout!* Introducing your host—international film star Gemma Weston!"

The studio audience applauds loudly. People whoop and whistle and a couple even scream for Gemma. A few of them are wearing costumes from their favorite Gemma movie roles!

"Hello, hello!" Gemma calls out. "Welcome

to night one of *Sing Out and Shout*. I think you are in for an entertaining evening. Here's how the show is going to work. We've invited six of your favorite celebrities to come out and sing tonight. Here's the catch: They aren't professional singers, so who knows what hidden talents or major upsets we'll see up on this stage. At the end of the night, after we tally the judges' votes and the votes from the live studio audience and the viewers at home, two contestants will be eliminated.

"Tomorrow, the remaining four will sing again, and again two contestants will be eliminated. Then on Sunday night, the final two contestants will sing against each other in an epic TV duet! The winner will donate the prize money to his or her favorite charity.

"Before our first contestant comes out, let me introduce you to our celebrity judges. You've already met one judge—me!"

The audience cheers wildly again. Then the spotlight and the camera swing over to the judges' table on the side of the stage.

"Judge number two knows a little bit about singing. Let's hear it for recording superstar Dustin Peeler!"

A huge roar, mixed with a few high-pitched shrieks, erupts from the audience. Then a chant begins: "Dustin! Dustin! Dustin!"

A close-up of Dustin appears on the screen. He waves and blows kisses to the crowd. It's incredible how natural he is at all of this. I wonder how many times Dustin has been on TV.

Gemma continues.

"Our third judge also knows quite a bit about music. Please welcome music critic Nicholas Campbell!"

There's less cheering for Nicholas. It seems like everyone is a little intimidated by him—just like I was. He does smile, though. Or at least, I *think* he smiles.

Gemma cuts to a commercial break. But it isn't a break for the studio audience. Here's a fun showbiz fact—TV hosts entertain their live audiences with jokes and stories while commercials run on your TV at home. This time

Gemma answers questions about *Alien Zombie Attack!*

"So when's the movie coming out?" asks a boy in the audience.

"Next month," Gemma tells him, smiling.

Huh. I hadn't realized it was coming out so soon!

She answers a few more questions—tells a teenage girl what it's like having to keep quiet when filming a movie to avoid spoilers, and how excited she is to host this TV show. Then we're back on air. Gemma counts down and the spotlight flashes up!

"And now it's time to meet our first

contestant," Gemma continues. "She's the president and CEO of Definite Devices, which just helped roll out the Definitely Sure Invisibility Kit! Please welcome my girl, NAT DEFINITE!"

If Nat is nervous, she doesn't show it. She gets up and flashes a giant smile at—who else?—Manny. Then she heads out of the green room and walks onstage like she's done this a million times.

As Gemma goes to her seat at the judges' table, Nat takes her place next to the microphone on the main stage and smiles.

"I'd like to thank Yamuna Stone for writing such a cool song for me and for all of you out there rooting and voting for me," she says as the applause dies down. "And Gemma for inviting me. And my friend Manny for helping make me famous." Next to me in the green room, Manny rolls his eyes. "This song is called *Now You See Me*."

Music blares from the speakers, and Nat begins singing:

"Now you see me, now you don't.
Can you find me? I'll bet you won't.
One spray now, and I'll disappear.
Another spray later, and I'm back here.
How do I vanish, then re-appear?
Well, lean in close and lend an ear,
Definite Devices and Sure Things, Inc.
Have worked together, now what do you think?
The Definitely Sure Invisibility Spray
Will make it seem like you went away.
No one will see you, and suddenly then,
With one more spray you'll be there again.
Now you see me, now you don't.
Now you see me, NOW YOU DON'T!"

The audience applauds and cheers. The judges scribble notes at their table. Then Gemma comes over and shakes Nat's hand.

Manny turns to me. "Good publicity," he whispers. I nod.

"She's a pretty good singer," I say back. "But not as good as you."

We turn our heads back to the TV monitor.

"That was very cool, Nat," says Gemma out onstage. "And that song's about the new product you and Sure Things, Inc. have just released, right?"

"That's right, Gemma," says Nat.

"Well, we'll be hearing from your business partners Manny Reyes and Billy Sure a little later in the show. Judges, what did you think?"

The camera dims on Gemma and turns to Dustin and Nicholas. Dustin is writing fast while Nicholas looks more relaxed. He has his arms crossed.

"Nat, I liked the emotion you brought to the song, you know?" Dustin says. Or at least, I *think* he says. A lot of people in the audience scream excitedly when he talks. "It showed a little bit about who you are, and that's what great singing is all about."

The camera turns toward Nicholas Campbell.

"I'd say it NEEDS SOME WORK," he says. Boos come from the audience.

"Well, I thought she was terrific," Gemma says, brightening the mood.

As Nat heads offstage and back to the green room, there's another commercial break. This time I start to feel really nervous. Gemma didn't tell us what order we're performing in! What if I'm next?

The commercial break ends, and Gemma speaks into her microphone.

"Our next contestant is a makeup artist," she says. "You've probably seen her videos. If not, you've definitely seen people inspired by them! Please welcome SARINA BROWN!"

Sarina gets up. Her curly brown hair bounces as she walks onto the stage carrying a makeup kit. I wonder if maybe her dog, Copper, will help her out like he does on her videos. That could be a lot of fun!

Out onstage Sarina stands up tall. "I'd also like to thank Yamuna Stone for writing such a great song," Sarina says. "She also gave me a great piece of advice. She said 'show the audience your special talent.' So I am going to put makeup on my face while I sing."

A low gasp comes from the audience.

"This should be interesting," I say to Manny. I mean, Nat didn't try to invent onstage or anything!

Sarina opens up her makeup kit and places it on a stool beside her. She is very organized. Then she starts singing:

"Some red on my lips, some blue for my eyes,
a blush of rose for my cheek,
Black for the lashes, my face looks so chic."

She continues, but—oh no. I don't know much about applying makeup, but I have a feeling this isn't how you're supposed to put it on. There's lipstick EVERYWHERE! Smeared on the microphone, on her neck, on her brushes ...

"Are you seeing what I'm seeing?" I ask Manny. "Does that look right to you?"

Up on the screen Sarina is attempting to put lipstick on her lips as she sings. It's like trying to hit a moving target. Red streaks of lipstick smear the side of her face.

She valiantly goes on.

"Subtlety and softness, those are the keys.
Blend it all slowly, the look is sure to please."

And now bright-blue eye shadow spreads across her forehead!

"Subtlety, huh?" I whisper to Manny. "I don't think this is going the way she had hoped."

Realizing this, the camera focuses in on Gemma. She looks a little panicked—but also, Gemma is a Hollywood pro. She dives under the judges' table and grabs a roll of paper towels. "Heads up!" she yells, then throws the paper towels at Sarina.

BOING!!

The paper towels hit Sarina on the head. Embarrassed, she rips off a piece of paper and starts wiping her face with it—but that only makes things worse! Now there are different colored smears all over her face!

Just when it looks like all hope is lost, there's a shout from the studio audience during a pause in the song. The voice sounds familiar. . . .

"Yes, Emily?" Gemma says to the voice.

Leave it to my sister, Emily, to FINAGLE HER WAY onto live TV!

"Gem, I have makeup remover in my bag right here," Emily says. She holds up the purple googly eyed purse to the camera and pulls out a bottle of what must be makeup remover. I had no idea they have special remover for that, but she throws it to Sarina and it works! Sarina's face becomes fresh and clean, makeup free.

I guess sometimes my annoying older sister can be, well . . . a *not* annoying older sister.

Despite all this, I'm impressed with Sarina. She never stops singing until her song is finished. She even ends on a high note! I almost forgot this was a singing competition.

"I liked the song," Dustin says, obviously feeling bad for Sarina. "Can everyone give Sarina major props for finishing that song?"

The audience cheers louder than they have yet!

Okay, that makes me feel better. Sarina's performance might have been a mess, but at least the crowd is being nice.

Gemma doesn't ask Nicholas Campbell what he thinks. That's kind of her. I don't really think he'd have anything nice to say.

Sarina returns to the green room.

"I liked the song too," I say to Sarina.

She smiles and nods, but I can see that she's not pleased.

Being the pro that she is, Gemma moves the show right along.

"Our next contestant is well-known to anyone who loves to cook—or eat! Please welcome TV chef extraordinaire, ARTHUR LING!"

Arthur gets up from the sofa and walks out onto the stage, pushing a rolling table in front of him. On the table sits a blender and a bunch of fruits and veggies.

"I'm also going to try to blend who I really am with my song. And speaking of blending ..."

On cue, the music starts. Arthur presses a button on the blender and the whirring noise adds to the music:

"Start with a banana, an orange, a pear,
Right in the blender, just drop them in there."

As he sings, Arthur drops fruit into the blender:

*"Some veggies come next. Did you think I'd forget
The carrots, the kale? But it gets better yet."*

In go the veggies, right in rhythm with the song. And again, the singing:

*"Tomato juice and yogurt, they are your next move.
They call this thing a smoothie, so come on . . .
MAKE IT SMOOTH!"*

He pours in tomato juice and yogurt, finishes his song, then turns off the blender, unhooks the pitcher, and gulps down half the smoothie.

I've never seen anything—and I mean *anything*—as slick as this. Arthur is really cool.

As if to demonstrate this further, he slams

the pitcher onto the table and smiles broadly through a greenish-orange smoothie mustache. Those ingredients all blended together can't taste good, but you'd never know it from Arthur's smile.

"Arthur Ling, everybody!" Gemma says, walking over to him.

Arthur picks up the pitcher and hands it to Gemma. She takes a drink and ends up with her own smoothie mustache. Of course, in typical Gemma style, she makes the SMOOTHIE 'STACHE look like a glamorous accessory!

The audience goes wild. I have to admit, that was really fun.

"It was all right," Nicholas Campbell says.

From him, I think that's a compliment!

"The song was cool, and the talent was even cooler," says Dustin.

"Thank you, Arthur!" Gemma says.

"That *was* pretty cool," I say to Manny, wondering how I'm going to combine my terrible voice with who I really am.

"Our next contestant is no stranger to Dustin

Peeler, and I'm guessing to our studio audience," Gemma says. "Please welcome backup dancer, MARCUS REBU!"

Marcus nods to us, then walks to the center of the stage. I wonder if he can sing as well as he dances.

He puts his head down and stands perfectly still. Unlike all the other contestants, he doesn't say a thing. He kind of looks like a wax figure! It's all very dramatic. Then the music starts and he begins dancing. He swirls his arms above his head, spins on his toes, and bends at the waist, whipping his head back and forth. He moves so fast I kind of wonder if he *did* pick up anchovies with his feet after all. These wild movements continue as he sings:

> *"Kick your leg, wave your arm,*
> *Moving your body won't do you any harm.*
> *Bend and shake and bop and weave,*
> *Keep your body moving, stick around, don't leave.*
> *Reach for the sky, dig into the ground,*
> *Don't stand still, keep moving around.*

Dance alone or dance with your friend,
Sing your song, now stretch and bend!"

WOW! I know as much about dancing as I do about singing—which is to say, not much—but his performance is incredible.

As if to further prove this, Marcus leaps high into the air, spins around, and lands in a squatting position. It looks so effortless. The music stops suddenly and all the lights go out.

When the lights come back on, the audience cheers.

"Now you all see why I won't perform without Marcus behind me," Dustin says. "I call him my secret weapon! But maybe next time on tour I'll bring him out for a little duet or two."

The show cuts to another commercial. I look around the room. The only people who haven't gone on yet are Manny and me. Which means that no matter what, ONE OF US is up after the commercial break.

I feel my arms start to shake, and my legs too. When the camera cuts back to Gemma, Manny whispers that everything will be okay. Isn't it weird that a few days ago I was the one convincing him to do the TV show in the first place?

"Okay," says Gemma. "Our next amateur singer is so famous, he doesn't need an introduction! But just in case, please welcome everyone's favorite kid entrepreneur, BILLY SURE!"

Chapter Nine

Manny's the Man

IT'S ME. I'M NEXT.

I get up and my legs feel like lead. I don't know how I'm going to sing—much less make it to the stage!

"Go get 'em, Billy," says Manny, patting me on the back. "You can do it!"

As I walk toward the stage, Yamuna Stone's words echo in my head: *Just go out there, use your special talent, and make yourself lovable.*

And Manny's: *You can do it!*

I just hope I can make it to the final round with him. . . .

I pause at the edge of the stage, take a deep

breath, and then walk out into the spotlight.

Smile, Billy! Smile! I remind myself. I force a smile onto my face, which I'm certain looks phony.

I wave to the cheering crowd as I walk toward Gemma, who stands in the middle of the stage, clapping.

Gemma hands me the microphone.

"Thanks, Gemma," I say. Or at least, I *think* I say. It kind of comes out as one word: THANKSGEMMA.

Geez, Billy, you're only on national TV, I tell myself.

I try again.

"I'm an inventor," I say. "Here's a song about inventing."

Okay, I might not exactly be Mr. Smooth.

The music starts. I hold onto my microphone. I try to find Emily and my parents or even Manny's parents in the audience, but I can't.

*"I'm so suuuuure about inventing;
I'm real suuuuure about creating."*

Okay! The first lines aren't so bad. No one is booing. . . . Things are going to be okay. . . .

"I can put together what doesn't seem plain.
If you ask me how I do it, I'd be glad to explain.
I am suuuuure about the inventions I'm bringing.
But I want to tell you now, I'm not suuuuure . . .
About SINGING!"

And once again, in exactly the same spot, as I belt the word "singing," my voice squeaks and *cracks*.

Oh no. What do I do? I'm NOT a singer!
I try singing the word "singing" again.
This time it's even worse:

"SIIIIIINGIIIING!!!!!"

CRaaaSH!

I stop singing. The loud noise shatters downward, kind of like a waterfall! There's a lot of lights, so I look around to see what happened, blinking back all that brightness. I feel dazed, when suddenly, a little girl in the first row yells, "MOOOOM! HE BROKE THE BACK MIRROR!"

The audience gasps, staring past me. I turn around onstage and my hands shake. I didn't just break any mirror, I broke *the* back mirror—the giant mirror that serves as a backdrop for the stage! It's shattered into what must be a million pieces.

What do I do? I know what I *want* to do. I

want to go home and forget all this.

Then more of Yamuna's words come back to me: *Show your humor and likeability to the audience and to the judges.*

What do I have to lose?

"Um," I address the audience. "I guess now is a good time to invent an UNBREAKABLE MIRROR."

Silence.

I'm done for.

Then a voice in the middle of the audience starts laughing. It's Emily!

Emily's laughter is contagious. Soon the rest of the audience breaks out into giggles and cackles too.

"Anyone have any tomatoes to throw at me?" I say. "I could really use them for my next invention. . . . Actually, that's why I chose to sing badly. We have budget cuts over at Sure Things, Inc., and I was told this is a good way to get vegetables thrown at you. . . ."

The audience howls! Even Gemma is laughing a lot. Dustin jumps up from the judges'

table, claps me on the back, and shouts, "My man!" The rest of the studio audience cheers along with him.

Did I do it? Did I make it to the next round? I have no idea—and Nicholas Campbell definitely doesn't say anything—but I decide this is probably the best opportunity to take a bow and leave, so I do.

As I walk offstage, I see Manny coming out.

"BREAK A LEG!" I tell him, feeling way too happy for a person who just broke a mirror on live TV.

Manny smiles. "See ya on the other side, partner," he says, and heads out.

I join the rest of the contestants back on the couch. No one says anything to me. I realize then how much I miss having Manny in the room, and Manny's only been gone for five seconds! I'm really glad we're doing the competition together. It makes me really want to come out on top, as team Sure Things, Inc.

I redirect my attention to the TV screen.

"Good evening, everyone. I believe you've

met my business partner, Billy. I'd like to tell you all about what I do at Sure Things, Inc."

Manny starts to sing:

"My name is Manny.
My skills are quite uncanny.
I can crunch the numbers, make a marketing plan-y.
I'm the business genius, I'm the mega-money man-ny.
There is no question, there is no doubt,
I am super psyched to be on Sing Out and Shout!
Billy invents a new product, then it's up to me.
How do we sell it; where should it be?
In big name stores or the mom and pops?
When my brain starts working, it never stops.
Internet only or in a store,
It really won't matter as long as we sell MORE!"

Okay, I'm not the only one who thinks Manny is incredible. Not only does the audience clap and cheer wildly even *more* than they did for Dustin Peeler!—but Manny gets the only standing ovation of the night! He's a SUPERSTAR!

The audience won't stop cheering. Then

Nicholas, Dustin, and Gemma join in the standing ovation, rising from their seats at the judges' table. The camera zooms around the audience, then back to Manny, then back to the audience again.

I feel really, really proud of him.

"Well, I think we know who the clear winner is tonight," says a voice at the judges' table.

It's Nicholas Campbell!

He just complimented my best friend, Manny!

"I have to say, I'm a little worried," says Dustin. "I hope that Manny sticks to business, because I don't know if I'm ready for the competition as a singer!"

Gemma doesn't say anything. For the first time all night, she doesn't need to. The audience screams it for her!

I'm smiling ear to ear. I might have had a terrible performance, but at least my best friend had a good one. Everyone in the green room is talking about Manny. "Did you see him? Did you hear him? Did you hear him SING?" Marcus says excitedly.

The only person who isn't celebrating, I notice, is Nat.

"You know, Billy, if that were my business partner, I'd be jealous," she whispers in my ear. "He's HOGGING all of the spotlight."

Instantly, my good mood feels crushed, but I don't respond. See, these are the kinds of things that make me not like Nat so much. Why did she have to say that? Why did she have to ruin such a happy moment? And, once I think about it for more than five seconds . . . why do I feel like she may be right?

I sigh. As happy as I am for Manny, I *do* feel a little jealous. No matter what happens, I will *never* sing that well.

When Manny reenters the green room, everyone applauds.

"I guess they liked me," Manny says in his usual humble way.

"Liked you?" I repeat. "Everyone loved you, Manny!"

But when I say it, I can't help but think

about what Nat said . . . maybe I am a little jealous after all.

Gemma appears on the TV screen.

"Well, the judges, the audience here in the studio, and all of you at home who've been texting your votes have made up your minds," she says.

I almost forgot how fast everything moves on live TV. Two of us are getting booted off the show tonight. And if I had to guess . . . I'd say one of them is probably me.

Oh no.

I can feel the tension among the contestants here in the green room. Everybody wants to move on to the next night of the competition. Only four of the six of us will.

"Nicholas, will you please read the results?" Gemma says.

The camera zooms in on Nicholas Campbell. But it zooms in a little too close, and all we see is his nose. (And his nose hairs . . . gross!) It reminds me of one of dad's paintings.

"We had a fun night here at *Sing Out and Shout*," Nicholas says. "From mediocre to okay to downright incredible. I'm pleased to announce the results."

The audience keeps on cheering. I might be mistaken, but I think I can hear people chanting, "Manny, Manny!" And it sounds like it's coming from the center of the audience—right where Mom, Dad, Emily, Mr. and Dr. Reyes are sitting. I don't know why, and I hate to think it, but that makes me feel a little sad.

I'm really nervous. I'm sure I'm going to be sent home. I was by far the worst singer. I mean, I even broke a mirror!

"Based on the votes here and our viewers at home, the two contestants tonight who won't be returning are . . ."

I brace myself.

"Sarina Brown . . ."

As much as I feel bad for Sarina, I can't say I'm surprised.

"And Arthur Ling."

No one, I mean no one, is more shocked than I am.

Arthur Ling? He was great. And he's really friendly. If I could, I probably would've voted for him. How is Arthur out of the competition while I'm still in?

Nat smiles at me. It's almost like she can read my thoughts.

"They must have felt sorry for you," she whispers in my ear again.

Note to self: Invent something that makes it so I do *not* hear what Nat whispers in my ear!

Nat's words get to me, and I barely notice what happens next. Although Arthur and Sarina may be out of the competition, they are very gracious about it. They shake everyone's hands and wish us good luck tomorrow.

"It was great meeting you all," Sarina says. "And, Billy, tell your sister I owe her one. Maybe even a one-on-one makeup tutorial. Ideally not on live TV." The contestants laugh.

After a few minutes of saying good-bye to everyone, Manny and I meet Mom, Dad, Emily, and Mr. and Dr. Reyes outside.

"You were amazing!" Emily says, running up to us.

Actually, scratch that. Emily doesn't even look at me. She says that to Manny!

Thankfully Mom seems to notice.

"You gave the most UNIQUE PERFOR-MANCE I've ever seen, honey," she says, beaming.

"Thanks," I reply. "I think."

Emily and Mom decide to take Gemma's

limo back home. Normally I'd be all for a limo ride too, but I think I've had enough of the celebrity life for today.

On the drive home, everyone talks about Manny's performance. "I wanted to be a singer when I was a kid!" Mr. Reyes says. "Like father, like son, huh?"

Manny shrugs.

I don't say much. Part of me can't believe that I've made it to the second night. Maybe Nat was right. Maybe people did feel sorry for me. But how long will that last? I'll never make it to the end and sing a duet with Manny—and even if I did, he'd just be better than me anyway.

That's the thing. Nat's other words haunt me. I *am* a little jealous of Manny's talent, and that makes me feel even worse.

I'm plotting how to make the STOP-HEARING-NAT-WHEN-SHE-WHISPERS-IN-YOUR-EAR invention when I remember something else—something Yamuna told me.

The winner of this show will use his or her special talent to win—and, you might be surprised

to hear this, but your special talent might not even be singing.

My special talent.

My special talent isn't singing, and it's not even making people laugh—my special talent is inventing.

Inventing!

That's when it hits me.

I'm going to invent my way to the finals!

Chapter Ten

Billy's Special Talent

OKAY, OKAY, LET ME EXPLAIN.

I have no doubt in my mind that Manny will get to the final round of *Sing Out and Shout*. Not after the way he sang on the first day.

And I know that I told him I'd try to get to the finale so we could sing together—for publicity for Sure Things, Inc.

I have to make it to the end for our company. Not to mention to ensure that the donation goes to the Young Inventors Organization!

So what I need to do . . . is invent a

MAGICAL MICROPHONE—a device that will make my voice sound better!

I sort of have mixed feelings about inventing the Magical Microphone. Is it cheating? I'm really against cheating, especially at school or playing board games. But I'm using my own special talent, and that's exactly what Yamuna told me to do, isn't it? I mean, I can't do what Sarina, Arthur, and Marcus can do, and they used their special talents onstage tonight. So technically it isn't cheating. After all, it's not my fault my special talent happens to be inventing.

I walk around my room Saturday morning, collecting materials that I can probably use for a Magical Microphone invention.

I find an old flashlight and attach a small battery pack. With a few changes, the flashlight works really well as a microphone—and, I think to myself, is kinda cool because it's a spotlight you can carry around! Then I add some more things I find around my room. When the microphone is ready, I dangle it over an old boom box and play different kinds of music. The microphone amplifies them.

"I love youuuuuu," plays a song by a woman with a raspy voice.

Then there's a hip-hop song that kind of makes me want to get up and dance.

I play another song and *REEEEE!!!* the boom box screeches out some screamo musics. "Move away from the mirror—your face has always looked like that," Emily shouts from her room.

"Ha-ha," I say. Leave it to Emily to come up with some kind of snarky comment about why she hears screaming coming from my room!

A couple of hours later the Magical Microphone is ready to test. There are small buttons on the side of it that program it to a different kind of singing voice. I hit the beat box and a funky rhythm comes pounding out. Well, I think. Here goes nothing!

"I'm so suuuuure about inventing;
I'm real suuuuure about creating."

MAGICAL MICROPHONE

I stop. I check my bedroom mirror. It's still there! No cracks!

I sing a few more lines, this time quieter. I sound good. Really good. If I sing with this microphone, Manny and I will probably make it to the final round together!

Later that afternoon, me, Emily, Mom, Dad, and Manny all pile into Dad's car. Manny's parents promise they'll catch up with us later. I ask Emily why she doesn't take Gemma's limo today, and she sticks out her tongue at me. I guess that's the best answer I'm going to get.

Today Emily is wearing a hat that is fully decorated with Christmas lights. There's even

a little Santa light. They blink on and off in different patterns. I don't remind her that it isn't Christmas.

"How are you feeling about tonight's show, Billy?" Dad asks.

"Pretty good, actually," I say, reaching down and feeling the Magical Microphone in my pocket.

Manny smiles. "I'm really glad," he says. "I was kinda worried that you'd be discouraged after yesterday. But hey, we'll get some more publicity for Sure Things, Inc. tonight, and hopefully even more at the finale tomorrow night!"

See? Even Manny says staying on the show is important.

"I've been practicing," I say, which isn't entirely untrue. "I think my singing will be a whole lot better tonight."

Emily rolls her eyes and shakes her head, causing several strands of blinking lights to fall off the hat and wrap around her ears.

At the studio Mom, Dad, and Emily head to the audience while Manny and I go to the green room. On the way, I notice Nat in the hallway talking to a man wearing a headset and carrying a clipboard.

As soon as Manny and I walk into the green room, Gemma comes over to Manny and gives him a BIG HUG.

"You sounded great last night," she says.

"Thanks," he replies.

Then she rushes off. Am I chopped liver? I start thinking about what exactly chopped liver is. Is it really that bad?

"Billy? You there?" Manny taps me on the shoulder a few minutes later. "It's time for you to meet with Yamuna for tonight's song."

I smile sheepishly at him and head over to the rehearsal room. Yamuna has a whole new set of lyrics for me for tonight's appearance.

"I have a really good feeling about these lyrics," I tell Yamuna after reading them.

"That's the spirit, Billy," she says. "Just show off your special talent. The song will take care of itself."

Then, just like the day before, the remaining contestants practice in the green room until the show starts. I tell Manny I'm too nervous to practice, so we go through his song a few times. Then Gemma sticks her head in. Once again, it's showtime!

Chapter Eleven

Magical Sounds

THE FOUR CONTESTANTS GATHER AROUND THE GREEN room monitor and the show begins. It's all exactly like yesterday—but this time, I'm not nervous. I feel good!

"Good evening and welcome to part two of *Sing Out and Shout!*" Gemma says from center stage. A few people in the green room clap, and I do too. "We have four contestants remaining. Each one will sing a brand-new song. Then you'll vote for your favorite to see who will be back tomorrow night.

"And now, please welcome our first contestant this evening—Marcus Rebu!"

Marcus nods to all of us. "SEE YA," he says, and dances his way onto the stage, spinning, leaping, and waving his arms around. Once he's onstage, he grabs his mic and starts singing:

"My moves are smooth, my song is sung.
Don't go away, 'cause I've just begun.
I express myself by doing a dance.
Come on, audience, give me a chance!"

Marcus's dance moves are incredible, but his voice sounds a little hoarse. Maybe he strained it too much yesterday. But even though his voice doesn't sound great, the judges—with the exception of Nicholas Campbell, who probably doesn't even love his teddy bear—love him.

Nat is up next. She seems even more charming than she did yesterday. The music begins and she sings her song:

"See a need, solve a problem, sell a product, oh yeah!
Inventing, inventing, inventing.
Now that success has come my way,
I'll do what I can to help other people,
Every morning, every evening, every day!"

Wow, she really seems sincere—which is good, because sometimes I think she's just in the inventing biz to crush on Manny. The judges like her again too.

"You have what we in the industry call 'presence,'" Dustin Peeler says.

"Charisma," Nicholas Campbell adds, nodding. He doesn't comment on her voice.

After a short commercial break, Gemma waltzes up to the stage, looking like a million dollars. She's wearing a SPARKLY GREEN DRESS, which kinda does literally look like it's made of a million dollars.

"You met him yesterday—you'll meet him

again today. Everyone put your hands up for Manny Reyes!"

At Manny's name, the crowd goes berserk. Everyone is cheering and screaming as Manny takes the stage. They're screaming louder than they did *after* Marcus and Nat's performances. Wow! He hasn't even started yet.

From the TV screen, I see Manny's cheeks turn a little red. He takes the microphone like a pro anyway and sings:

"Working as a team is the only way to go.
Sharing with my partner is the only way I know.
To run a big-time business, and be a big-time friend,
We have to work together—beginning, middle, and end!"

When he's done, a group of kids in the first row hold up **WE LOVE YOU, MANNY** signs. The judges give Manny another standing ovation. No question about it. Absolutely, 100 percent, no question. Manny is going to the finals!

I'm the only one left to sing, so I leave the green room and head to the stage. My heart pounds. My stomach tightens. I wasn't nervous before, but for some reason, now I am. I reach into my pocket and grab the Magical Microphone.

Gemma walks to center stage. "And now our final contestant—everyone, please welcome Billy Sure!"

I walk to the middle of the stage. The lights go out. I use the darkness to secretly pull out the Magical Microphone.

Then the spotlight hits me. Okay, I think. This is it. Now or never. Even more than before, I have to make it to the end with Manny.

I bring the Magical Microphone up to my mouth and start singing. . . .

Boom-chika-bop-bop, boom. Boom-chika-bop-bop, boom.

Wait—what? Those aren't the lyrics. . . . I look into the crowd, feeling flustered, when I realize the crowd is cheering and clapping along! I quickly hit another button on the microphone. I can't beat-box my entire way through this song.

"Building in my workshop, working at my bench,
Have you heard of the Stink Spectacular? Man,
that stench!"

Only I must have hit the wrong button, because
this time I'm belting it like an opera singer!
   The audience bursts out laughing.
   I fumble, press another button, and continue:

"What's that you say? What's the invention?
It's the Next Big Thing, and it's on a competition!"

Okay, now my voice sounds really deep and smooth, like some old time jazz singer. And the crowd cheers. I think I see one of the kids in the front row write my name on the poster, so now it says WE LOVE YOU, MANNY AND BILLY. I admit it: I'm starting to have fun!

Switch number four. Let's see what this does:

"So that's my story, that's my song.
I hope I did it right; I hate it when I'm wrong.
The time has gone so quickly; I wonder where it went.
Hey, that gives me an idea! Time to go invent!"

This time my voice sounds perfect. As good as Manny's. Smooth, beautiful, on key—I take a bow.

There's a standing ovation!

"Billy Sure, everyone!" Gemma shouts. "Wow,

that was fantastic. Shall we get the judges' thoughts?"

Dustin Peeler nods a lot. He doesn't say much—just nods. It sounds like: "Billy Sure" — nod—"you, *man*, you" —nod—"you *killed* it, man!" More nodding.

Gemma can't stop smiling.

And then she turns to Nicholas Campbell.

Nicholas stares right at me. He looks kind of like the grim reaper—he's got dark hair that falls everywhere and giant eyes. I prepare myself for the worst.

"Well, I didn't hate it," Nicholas says. He then breaks out into a smile! "I *loved* it."

What? Wait—what? Nicholas Campbell—*the* Nicholas Campbell—loved my performance?

"By far and away the most original and entertaining performance I've seen on *any* reality show," Nicholas continues. "BRAVO!"

At this, the audience cheers. "Bravo! Bravo! Bravo!"

Wow. I never knew you could be loved this much by a live audience.

I bow timidly, then hurry offstage into the green room.

Immediately, I'm met by Yamuna, who gives me a big hug.

"That was perfect, Billy!" she says. "Your range of sounds—hilarious! Stunning. You did it!" Her smile is huge.

"Thanks," I say.

The other contestants gather around me.

"You got some smooth style, there, Billy," says Marcus.

"Who knew that the boy inventor had other talents?" asks Nat.

The crowd around me breaks up, and I see Manny sitting alone in the corner. I go over to him.

"That went well," I say. "Maybe there's still a chance you and I will make it to the finals together."

Manny stands up and looks me in the eye.

"Billy," he says. His voice is calm. Manny is usually calm, but this is calm even for Manny. "You can't sing. We both know that. What are you hiding from me?"

I look down. I don't know what made me think I could fool Manny.

I feel bad not telling Manny about my invention, but I'm not sure the time is right to reveal it.

Manny sits back down. On the TV screen, Gemma heads back out onto the stage to announce tonight's winners. The mood in the green room is pretty tense.

All of the contestants are gathered around the big screen. What's weird is that there must be a secret camera here somewhere, because occasionally the TV flashes to show us waiting. Nat grabs Marcus's hand. "Let's all hold hands so we look united," she says. It's a nice gesture, but I have a feeling she says that because Manny is on her other side!

"Well, once again, all our performers were fabulous, don't you agree?" Gemma says.

The studio audience goes wild.

"A very entertaining day," says Nicholas Campbell.

"Seeing all these great performances reminds me why I got into music in the first place," says Dustin Peeler.

"It is now time to announce which two contestants will be returning TOMORROW NIGHT!" Gemma announces.

I'm holding hands with Manny, on the side that Nat isn't. I squeeze his hand nervously, but he doesn't do anything back.

"And those two contestants are . . . well, I can't say I'm surprised." Gemma laughs. "Manny Reyes . . . and Billy Sure!"

Everyone's hands break apart. I look over at Manny, hoping to celebrate a Sure Things, Inc. win. But Manny looks puzzled, like he's trying to figure something out.

Up on the TV screen, everyone is clapping and cheering rhythmically.

"Well, what are you guys waiting for?" Nat asks. "Get out onstage! Everyone is asking for the winners!"

Manny and I hurry out onstage and the crowd gets even louder. Half the crowd is cheering, "Billy!" while half the crowd is cheering, "Manny!" It's surreal. I don't know why, but I'd expected them all to be cheering, "SURE THINGS, INC.!"

I wave to the crowd, not sure I really want to say anything right now. Gemma wraps up the show.

"That's it for tonight. Be sure to tune in tomorrow for an epic Sure Things, Inc. showdown!"

And we're off the air.

"You guys were awesome," Gemma says, a little too brightly. "See you tomorrow!"

Manny and I meet up with Mom, Dad, and Emily—who gushes about how Gemma complimented the Christmas lights on her hat—outside the theater. Mr. and Dr. Reyes stand there too, each wearing a shirt that says "MANNY IS OUR SUN" with Manny's face in the sun.

"I never knew you had so much talent, honey!" Mom says to me as we get into the car.

Emily and Dad join in with choruses of "you were great!" and "no broken mirrors!" I, however, say nothing. I ride the entire way home in silence, wondering what Manny is wondering.

Chapter Twelve

The Final Word

I TOSS AND TURN THAT NIGHT, BOTH FROM excitement about the next day's finals and from worry. I'm really happy the Young Inventors Organization is getting our prize money no matter which one of us wins, and that Sure Things, Inc. will get another day of publicity, but I need to tell Manny what's going on. Manny is my best friend!

I finally drift off to sleep and have a dream in which an opera singer, a gospel singer, and a hip-hop star chase me across the *Sing Out and Shout* stage, all trying to get the Magical

Microphone out of my hands. They're screaming at me.

I wake up screaming too and then relax,
remembering it was just a dream. Nothing to
worry about but nerves. Luckily, we have to get
to the TV studio super early the next day, so I
don't have much time to dwell on my dream.
And I don't see Manny before he gets there
because he drives over with his parents. The
car ride to the TV studio is pretty quiet. Even
Emily's latest hat—a tall tower of a cowboy hat,
a straw hat, and a baseball cap sewn together
and sitting on top of one another—doesn't spur
any conversation.

I just need to get through tonight's show.
But Mom and Dad seem kind of quiet too. And
even a little bit tense?

I'll just be really glad later tonight when
this is all over.

As soon as I get to the studio, I see Manny
and Gemma.

"You guys ready?" Gemma asks.

"Ready!" Manny and I say in unison.

"Okay, so tonight's competition is going to be a little different from the last two nights," Gemma explains, scribbling something down. "The two of you will sing a karaoke-style duet onstage together. The lyrics—written by Yamuna, of course—will be on a screen for you to read. Part of the fun is that there's no practicing."

She looks at us, as if waiting for a response. I don't have one, so I shrug. Manny doesn't say anything either.

"All right, then," says Gemma, pretending we just shouted from the top of the world that we love *Sing Out and Shout*. "Good luck, you two! We'll be on shortly. Enjoy yourselves in the green room!"

Interestingly enough, although there are

fewer people in here, the green room is packed with food today—even more than before. In addition to all the food, candy, and soda that is out, there are cakes decorated to look like Sure Things, Inc. inventions. "Manny, check this out," I say, eyeing cake that's decorated with some kind of DISAPPEARING REAPPEARING ICING thats inspired by one of our first products, Disappearing Reappearing Make-Up.

I try to make small talk a few more times before we're called back onstage, but Manny doesn't want to talk. Maybe he's nervous about tonight's performance, or maybe he's still suspicious of why my voice sounded better last night.

But before I get a private moment to tell him about the Magical Microphone, it's time for the show to start. "Welcome to the third and final night of *Sing Out and Shout!*" Gemma announces from center stage. "Who knew that the faces behind Sure Things, Inc. were such a musical duo?"

The audience applauds. Gemma is a pro. She announces Manny and me, then goes on to tell some jokes. She also recaps some highlights from the past few days. I would have never guessed this on Friday, but I've had a lot of fun.

"So, now ladies and gentlemen, please welcome Billy and Manny, who will be performing a brand-new duet called 'The Best of Best Friends,' written by Yamuna Stone!" Gemma announces.

Manny and I walk onstage side-by-side, each holding a microphone. I'm sure, like me, Manny just wants this all to be over. After all, I did have to convince him to do this TV show in the first place!

The kids in the front row all have their signs again—I'm surprised they managed to get tickets for another night. A few other people have signs too. I notice Emily in the audience because of her hat. *Just another performance,* I tell myself as I switch on the Magical Microphone. Then music swells and lyrics appear on a big screen in front of us. My lyrics are first:

"What's it mean to be a pal? What's it mean to be
a friend?
It means sticking together, beginning to end."

Then it's Manny's turn:

"Friends are one thing, good friends another,
But being best friends is like having a brother."

The music plays on as we try to catch the beat.
Then my lyrics come up again, and I know it's
my turn, so I sing:

"Best friends are always honest, they never tell a lie."

And then it happens. As I sing the line,
the Magical Microphone glitches. It
CRACKLES! and **SQUEALS!** sending out a high-
pitched tone! Oh no, oh no, oh no—my
voice changes back to its normal, horri-
ble sound. Then it cracks, like it did the

first time I sang! I try to keep going.

"They help each other always, they're always there to tryyyyyy . . .

No such luck. **SMASH!**

A glass of water that had been sitting on a stool on the side of the stage shatters, sending shards of glass and water flying! The broken glass doesn't hit anyone, but the pieces fall all over the floor!

The audience laughs. They think I'm pulling the same stunt I did last night, where I'll be good in the end. Honestly? I *hope* that's what I'm doing, but I don't know!

As Manny sings his part, I try my best to switch the Magical Microphone on again fast.

Fortunately this time a nice singing voice comes out.

"Manny and Billy, the best of best friends,
Working and playing, then doing it again.
Billy and Manny, the best of best friends.

*Together at the start, together . . . at . . . the . . .
eeeeeeend!"*

The lights drop.

"A GREAT DUET!" Gemma shouts, coming up to join us onstage as the lights come back on. "The finest of songs. A big thank-you to Yamuna Stone, who wrote every song you heard during the last three nights. We're gonna go to a commercial break while the judges choose the winner of *Sing Out and Shout!* We'll be right back!"

The camera operators motion that they've stopped filming, and Gemma walks toward the studio audience.

"Well, what did you think?" she asks them. She tries to poll them to see who they think will be the winner—but it's right down the middle. I have that nervous feeling in my stomach. I didn't want to take the spotlight from Manny. I wanted to use my special talent. I wanted the Young Inventors Organization to get the donation. I wanted

Sure Things, Inc. to get the publicity from both me and Manny appearing on all three days of the show. But, if I'm being honest, I guess I wanted to share the spotlight with Manny too. Nat got to my head. I did feel jealous and now I feel bad.

After Gemma's little poll, Manny turns and hurries back to the green room. I chase after him.

When we are both alone in the green room (checking to make sure the hidden video camera isn't on), Manny turns to me.

"I *know* what you did, Billy," he says. "I heard that glitch. I heard your voice change, then change back again. I *knew* it the instant I heard you sing last night."

What can I do? I have to tell him what's going on. Like the song says, we are the best of best friends. But Manny's not finished.

"Did you invent something to help you sing better?" he asks. "Some kind of special microphone?"

I don't know what to say. Is Manny happy we

135

both made it to the final round or upset with me?

"Well, I wanted us both to get to the final round and so I used my special talent, and I guess I was also a litle jealous," I begin when Gemma sticks her head into the green room.

"We're coming back on, guys," she says, absolutely giddy. "Get ready!"

We have no choice. Before I can tell Manny the whole story, we leave the green room to go back out onstage, and I'm shocked to see Nat standing in the hallway talking to one of the show's producers.

What's she doing here? I think. *She's not competing tonight.*

I don't have a lot of time to think about that, though, because a few moments later we're back on air, and back onstage with Gemma.

"The judges have made their final decision," Gemma says, more seriously than she's said anything on the whole show. "Folks, we have a winner of *Sing Out and Shout!*"

There's thunderous applause.

Gemma continues.

"For his versatility, humor, excellent show-manship, and most importantly, his ability to entertain, please give it up for our winner . . ."

I take a deep breath.

"BILLY SURE!"

It's like a madhouse. Everyone cheers. People hold up posters that say I'M SURE FOR BILLY SURE! and confetti falls down all around me. I hadn't noticed it before, but the former contestants are in the seats in front. They cheer loudest of all.

I wave my hand and the music stops. Then I switch on the Magical Microphone and hold it up to my mouth.

"I have a confession to make," I say. I wish I'd told Manny before it had to be on live TV, but nothing much I can do about that now. "This is a Magical Microphone, which I invented. It turns any bad singer into a good one. I'm sorry, everyone. The real winner here is Manny.

To my great shock, Manny snatches the microphone from my hand!

"Billy, you would have won anyway with how you always made the audience laugh," Manny says. "Besides, the real winner isn't me and it isn't you. It's Sure Things, Inc. and all of our customers! Say hello to Sure Things, Inc.'s Next Big Thing—the MAGICAL MICROPHONE!"

Manny displays my invention for all to see. "Billy used his special talents to invent the Magical Microphone, which takes the worst of singers and turns them into superstars. Billy, please demonstrate."

I smile. Manny just turned this into a win for everyone. That's reason #888 why I'm super glad he's my best friend and business partner!

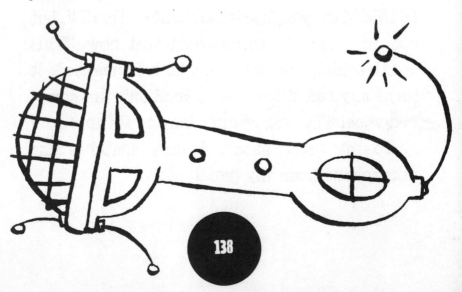

The lyrics to our duet come back up, and I sing a little bit with my own voice.

Terrible. No surprise there.

"Now Billy will use the Magical Microphone," Manny says. He switches it on and hands it to me. I sing the final lines of our song, and, of course, I sound FANTASTIC.

"And there you have it," Manny says when I finish. "Sure Things, Inc.'s Next Big Thing. But in this case, all proceeds for the Magical Microphone will be split between the charities our fellow contestants have sung for. Thanks, everyone! Good night!"

Just like that, the cameras go off. The lights dim. The show is over.

Gemma walks up to us holding the TV show rankings on her smartphone. She breaks out into a smile. "I have to say, if a TV show wants high ratings, all they have to do is put you two on it! Thanks, Sure Things, Inc."

She shakes our hands as Emily and Mr. and Dr. Reyes join us onstage. Marcus, Sarina, and Arthur come up too. They are thrilled that their charities will get so much money from the sales of the Magical Microphone. Meanwhile, Mom and Dad stay seated—I see them talk about something quietly. They keep whispering and looking in our direction.

"And now it's time to grab food with Em." Gemma beams. "I know the perfect late night sushi place!"

Emily smiles. Then, arm in arm, Gem and Em head off to the restaurant—in Gemma's limo, no doubt.

How is it that I win a reality TV show, and my sister ends up winning for real?!

"Thanks for everything," I say to Manny.

He shrugs. "No problem. I just wish you had told me what you were planning. I knew something was going on, but I didn't know what. We should always tell each other about things like Magical Microphones or feeling jealous. We're a team. NO MATTER WHAT."

"*Really?* No matter what?" comes a voice from behind us.

I spin around and see Nat walking out onto the stage.

"I definitely didn't expect that ending—especially not on a TV show sponsored by my company, Definite Devices," Nat says.

What?

"*Sing Out and Shout* is sponsored by Definite Devices?!" I yelp. I look up at the TV monitor where the end credits of the show are running. It hits me now that I've never seen the credits. Why would I have? I was *on* the show! But sure enough—Nat Definite is listed as a producer!

"You planned this all along!" I shout. "That's why you said you'd be jealous of Manny if you were me! You planted that seed in my head. You did all this—put on this whole show, went through all this trouble—just to get us to argue, and to get Manny to join your company. Again!"

Nat sighs. "You're right," she admits. She sounds bored. "Don't worry. Gemma and the rest didn't know. All this just ended up being great publicity for Sure Things, Inc. Obviously, not my intention."

My head is still spinning from all this. But Nat goes on.

"You may have won this round, but mark my words, Billy Sure. Now that the Definitely Sure Invisibility Kit is on the market, our partnership is over. We're competitors now. And as you just proved, Billy, competitors will use their special talents to succeed, and my special talent is thinking up ways to steal Manny away. I'll say it again: Manny *will* be joining our company. Just you wait."

"You're going to be waiting a long time, Nat," Manny says. "Because that is simply NOT GOING TO HAPPEN."

Manny smiles, and Nat leaves the stage.

"You know, Billy," he says. "Seriously though. This Magical Microphone? It might be one of your best ideas yet."

I smile. This is the Manny I know and love. He's not fazed by Nat at all. He's just thinking about the Next Big Thing.

"Definitely the best marketing launch ever, partner," I say.

Later, Mom hands Manny and me each a bouquet of flowers—and a gift card to the arcade. Dr. Reyes hands us each a foot brush. I never knew you needed to brush your feet.

"We're so proud of you both," Mom says. Dr. Reyes beams too.

Then Mom's expression suddenly turns serious. She looks at Dad.

"I don't want to rain on your parade, Billy," Dad begins, "but something is brewing and your mom and I might be making a big announcement soon."

"What do you mean?" I ask.

Dad continues. "Let's just say that I am going to have to start learning Italian."

Oh no. I *completely* forgot all about Mom and Dad's conversations about Italy last week!

It must be true. Dad must be moving to Italy.

What about Mom?

And what about me and Emily?

What if my whole life is about to change?

Want more Billy Sure?
Sure you do!
Take a sneak peek at the next
book in the Billy Sure
Kid Entrepreneur series!

BILLY SURE
KID ENTREPRENEUR
AND THE EVERYTHING LOCATOR

INVENTED BY LUKE SHARPE
DRAWINGS BY GRAHAM ROSS

My name is Billy Sure. I'm thirteen years old. I'm also a seventh grader at Fillmore Middle School and—oh yeah, I just got home from a busy day at the office.

At the office? you might ask. Along with my best friend (and CFO) Manny Reyes, we run the invention company Sure Things, Inc. Sure Things, Inc. has come out with all kinds of cool inventions you've probably heard of, including the All Ball, the Sibling Silencer, and our latest creation, the Magical Microphone.

"Well, you're home early for a change," Mom says as I walk into the kitchen.

"Yeah, it's kind of in-between time for Manny and me," I explain. "We're still testing out the Magical Microphone, and the Really Great Hovercraft Toy and the Invisibility Kit are just hitting stores now, so the pressure is off for the moment to invent something new."

"Great!" says Mom. "Then you can help me set the table for dinner."

As I help Mom put out plates, silverware,

napkins, and cups, I think about how great it has been having her home for so long. My mom spends a lot of time away for work. You know how my job as an inventor is cool? My mom has a cool job too—she's a spy! She protects the whole country. Although she's home now, she can be called into a spy mission at any time. So I'm thankful just to have her here.

My dad is an artist. He paints all kinds of, um, "unique" things. Like my dog Philo's nostrils, whiskers, and butt. He recently put up all his work in an art gallery and it was a big success.

Oh no—that's when I remember. Dad's art gallery. A few days ago, I overheard a conversation between my mom and dad, though I don't think they know I heard them. An art lover offered Dad a job to paint for her—all the way in Italy!

I know, I know. I should be really happy for him. But if Dad is away, and Mom suddenly gets called off to save the world, who will take care of my sister, Emily, and me?

"You're awfully quiet tonight, Billy," Mom says.

"Yeah," I say, placing a fork on the table. What can I say? I can't let on that I overheard Mom and Dad's conversation.

Mom is unfazed.

"Well, I know something that will perk you right up—tonight's dinner," she says. "We're having the Sure family secret ultra-cheesy lasagna recipe!"

"The Sure family secret ultra-cheesy lasagna recipe?" I ask.

I think after living in this house for thirteen years I would know if there was a Sure Family secret ultra-cheesy lasagna recipe!!!

"Oh, well, you may know it by a different name," Mom says. I can see a sly grin spreading across her face. "Takeout."

Okay, now that I know. Normally I would get a kick out of Mom's little joke. I'd also be super psyched about eating takeout, especially Italian food takeout. But the fact that it's, well, Italian, makes me nervous. Is tonight the night we find out Dad is moving to Italy?

A few minutes later Dad and Emily join Mom and me at the table.

I immediately notice that Emily is not wearing a hat.

If this sounds strange to you, let me explain. My sister always has a "thing" —something she gets into, like wearing giant hats or talking in a British accent—that is absolutely the 100 percent most important thing in the whole wide world to her at the time. Emily's things come from nowhere. And then they fade into nowhere fast.

So seeing Emily hatless? That means her next thing will reveal itself soon.

I can hardly wait.

The meal proceeds quietly, and my thoughts turn to an upcoming meeting of the Fillmore Middle School Inventors Club. I started the club and kind of stepped back when things got extra busy at Sure Things, Inc. But I really like the way club has become a place for kids to hang out and test their inventing skills.

I'm thinking about going to the next meeting, when Dad speaks up.

"I have an announcement to make," he says.

I stop chewing.

Oh no. This is it.

"As Emily learned by writing thank-you notes to everyone who came to the art exhibit, my show was a success," Dad says. "In fact, it was so successful that an art dealer in Italy named Tali DeCiso contacted me and asked me to do a series of paintings for her!"

I put my fork down, feeling sick, just as Emily squeals.

"That is so fantastic, Dad!" says Emily. "It's amazing! And to think, that happened because of the thank-you note I wrote."

"Um, I think your father's paintings had a little something to do with it as well, Emily," Mom points out.

"It's really a once in a lifetime opportunity," says Dad.

This is it. Here it comes. Dad's big

announcement that he's moving to Italy.

"Your mom and I have talked it over, and we've come to the conclusion . . . ,"

Dad pauses. I brace myself for the worst.

"The entire Sure family is moving to Italy!"

Did you LOVE reading this book?

Visit the Whyville...

Where you can:

- ○ Discover great books!
- ○ Meet new friends!
- ○ Read exclusive sneak peeks and more!

Log on to visit now!
bookhive.whyville.net

Looking for another great book?
Find it
IN THE MIDDLE.

Fun, fantastic books for kids
in the in-beTWEEN age.

IntheMiddleBooks.com